Mail Ord
The Reluctant Bride

By
Faith Johnson

Clean and Wholesome Western Historical Romance

Table of Contents

Unsolicited Testimonials

By **Glaidene Ramsey**
⭐⭐⭐⭐⭐ I so enjoy reading Faith Johnson's stories. This Bride and groom met as she arrived in town. They were married and then the story begins.!!!! Enjoy

By **Voracious Reader**
⭐⭐⭐⭐⭐ "Great story of love and of faith. The hardships we may have to go through and how with faith, and God's help we can get through them" -

By **Glaidene's reads**
⭐⭐⭐⭐⭐ "Faith Johnson is a five star writer. I have read a majority of her books. I enjoyed the story and hope you will too!!!!!"

By **Kirk Statler**
⭐⭐⭐⭐⭐ I liked the book. A different twist because she wasn't in contract with anyone when she went. She went. God provided for her needs. God blessed her above and beyond.

By **Amazon Customer**
⭐⭐⭐⭐⭐ Great clean and easy reading, a lot of fun for you to know ignores words this is crazy so I'll not reviewing again. Let me tell it and go

By **Kindle Customer**
⭐⭐⭐⭐⭐ Wonderful story. You have such a way of showing people that opposite do attack. Both in words and action. I am glad that I found your books.

FREE GIFT

Just to say thanks for checking our works we like to gift you

Our Exclusive Never Before Released Books

100% FREE!

Please GO TO

`http://cleanromancepublishing.com/gift`

And get your FREE gift

Thanks for being such a wonderful client.

Chapter One

The McKee Ranch was a staple landmark in the quaint town of Crow's Tooth. It had been around since the founding of the town, which at its beginning had been prosperous and bustling. But, as the town aged, the surrounding mountains slowly crept their way in, dandelions and weeds scaring out the farmers like the canary from the nearby mines. It seemed each generation feared the woods more and more than the previous one.

Great Granddaddy McKee had built the dining room table that Luella and her daddy sat at. The wood had been pieced together while the houses throughout the town went up, oak gleaned from the scrap wood of buildings.

At one point, the table had been filled with life. Generations used to sit around it. However, the McKee family had fallen to the same fate as the rest of the town. Most of them had succumbed to their fear of the woods, and parted from the Appalachian mountains to the 'safety' of the big city.

Or to the 'safety' of death.

That had been the fate that fell upon the eldest of the McKees. Louis, who should have been the proud patriarch of the McKees, letting Daddy McKee rest on the rocking chair and overlook plump livestock, was now six feet under. In the wake of his heartless execution, he had left behind thousands of dollars in debt to the poker tables, run by the Galloway boys, for his family to clean up.

The failing town had made a dent in Daddy McKee's health, already in shambles from age and from working since he could walk. With the execution of his heir and the heartbreak of his wife's passing soon after, he didn't have to rely on time or the sun or work to age him. His skin wrinkled like his grandfather's, helped by countless burns and accidents with cotton gins from his youth.

The only thing keeping him young was his slowly-shrinking herd of cattle and his daughter, Luella. She looked just like her daddy, who looked just like his mama. Round eyes with pronounced cheekbones. Her puffy brown hair was always worn in a plait, which Daddy McKee would do for her on rainy mornings. The gap between her two front teeth kept her youthful and the sunlight radiating from her.

As Daddy McKee aged, Luella had taken up most of his responsibilities. She cared for the cattle, milking them and pressing understanding kisses to their broad foreheads when they couldn't produce as much milk as they normally had. The hay bales in Crow's Tooth were kept by the same men who owned the poker tables to which the McKees were indebted.

She'd taken up cooking as soon as her mother had passed. It was filling all the same, but lacked the flavors that only mamas could truly add. Red beans and rice sat at the table, along with a cheap cut of meat that would barely feed one, let alone two farmhands.

Great Granddaddy's table shook under Daddy McKee's knife as he cut Luella a larger slice than himself. The meat is tough, but it'll nourish well. The two sat at the once-bustling table, which held so few now.

Daddy McKee had spent the day in town. He had been abnormally silent upon returning home, guilt swirling above his head like a summer storm.

"What's wrong, Daddy? Don't tell me the Galloways gave you trouble."

Daddy McKee chuckled. "Nah, they didn't give no trouble." He swallowed some of his food. "Dinner's good, dumplin.'"

It was not the best meal, far from it in fact, but the compliment delayed whatever bad news Daddy McKee was working up the courage to tell. It obviously weighed on him, the devil massaging his shoulders.

"I saw Mrs. Paula today," Daddy McKee started. Mrs. Paula sold pies on Sundays after church. Her husband, Mr. Galloway, was the man the McKees had become indebted to. The married couple had not spoken in years. No one in the town dared to talk of the separation. "She made me an offer I'd be a fool to reject."

Luella remained quiet. She watched as her daddy set his silverware down. He folded his hands together and looked at his daughter seriously. "She's got a cousin who lives out in Oregon. Mr. Jesse Lee. He's lookin' for a wife."

Luella's stomach sank.

"And you know how Mrs. Paula loves you. She spoke you up in her letter to him. He's..." Either a laugh or a choked cry emerged from his throat. "He's willin' to pay off our debts in exchange for you to come out West with him."

Luella supposed that it would always come down to it. She was older enough to be a wife. Stay-at-home daughters were few and far between. And the cows were close to showing bone. At only twenty-three, it was high and time.

And here sat poor Daddy McKee, who had lost one child and, to make up for the boy's digressions, had to lose his other.

"Who's gonna help you on the farm?" Luella asked.

"Mr. Jesse Lee has a cousin who needs to be taught some lessons, be taught some kindness. You know there ain't no better teacher than an ol' heifer."

Luella bit the inside of her cheek. The food before her looked as unappetizing as it was. She pushed a red bean about. She'd been starving just moments earlier from her hard day's work. Now, her appetite had been satiated by her looming future.

"It'll all work out," Daddy McKee promised. He gave his daughter a reassuring smile that would have worked under any other circumstances. "And it's not like we won't ever see each other again. Once I get your brother's debts settled, I'll come out to be with you."

Luella remained unconvinced. She swallowed heavily, reality thick in her throat.

"Are you sure I can't stay here? Maybe Mister…"

"Mr. Lee doesn't want nothin' to do with our town," Daddy McKee stated, firm and regretful. "I can't be askin' the gift horse for more graciousness than we're already gettin.'"

Air collected in the left side of Luella's cheek, puffing it out while she looked down. The breath left her, shallow and shaky. She wanted to get up from the table, not finish her meal, and leave her father to sit in his decision by himself.

But her days at her Granddaddy's table were numbered. She'd probably never see the worn oak that wobbles when the meat is too tough to cut through again.

"You're gonna be livin' better than you could imagine," Daddy McKee continued. Damage control. His whole life revolved around damage control. "Mrs. Paula says his house has a porch that wraps around, with a maid and a cook who comes on Sundays. You're gonna get to have everythin' I couldn't give you. Just like I prayed for." His voice cracked and shook.

His remorse gave Luella enough strength to bring another red bean to her lips. She'd need the energy around the cows tomorrow. She'd need the energy to forgive her Daddy while she slept.

Chapter Two

Luella wore her Sunday best. Once a distinct pink, it was now dusty like her windowsill. Little bows decorated the garment, along with a speckling of lace. It had been her mama's and rarely worn by the late woman. Despite her love for Daddy and dancing, she could barely bring herself to leave the ranch house.

The Sunday best and tomorrow's traveling clothes were the only things of Luella's not packed away. She'd prayed extra times over at church this morning. For a favorable trip, for Daddy's health, and for her betrothed to please, *please* be tolerable.

The McKees walked through the town, side by side. The air was kept crispy by birdsong and pine trees. Old oaks stretched their branches into the village as if to eavesdrop on the latest human trends.

In Luella's hands rested a platter of scones. Strawberry rhubarb, to match the summer weather. Mrs. Paula was always insistent on baking pies for any occasion. The scones would be for tomorrow morning.

Daddy McKee treated himself for the walk. He used a gnarled cane to assist him, each notch like sunken, closed eyes.

The Galloways owned the nicest house in the town. A birdhouse sat out front, which Mrs. Paula watched while her pies cooled in the windows. It took time for Daddy McKee to climb their stairs and knock on the solid door.

The door was answered by the pearled Mrs. Paula. Her hair sat perfectly, despite the humidity. Luella worried, for a brief moment, how much her hair had frizzed on the way to dinner.

It did not matter. The deal was done, and there was no one she had to impress.

"The McKees! Always such *dee-light* to see you both," Mrs. Paula smiled so wide the apples of her cheeks almost tumbled off.

"Nice to see you too, Mrs. Paula."

Luella chimed in alongside Daddy McKee, "Always a blessin' to see you too, Mrs. Paula."

They were led through the shotgun house out to the backyard, where a table was set. Rising from his chair must be none other than Mr. Jesse Lee.

He was nothing like what Luella had imagined of the man. She had expected him to be ugly, if she was being honest. Why else would a man *order* a wife he had never met?

But this man before her was tall and broad, with angled features and a trim waist. He wore a trim waistcoat perfectly tailored to his figure. How he stood the heat in such a collection of garments was a mystery to Luella.

Mrs. Paula shared introductions with her company. Luella briefly caught her name rolling off Mrs. Paula's tongue before her hand was in the man's. A brief shake, as if she were a magnolia flower, before he pressed a forward yet polite kiss to her knuckles.

She *was* to be married to him.

"Pleasure to meet your acquaintance, Miss McKee," he said, voice rough with a kind edge. "How do you do?"

"Fine, thank you," Luella responded. How stiff of a question. How stiff of a man. Perhaps *this* was the reason Mrs. Paula had to become invested in his dating life. "And you?"

"Better now."

The response was a bit corny, and Luella sucked on her tongue to keep from casting a glance over at her daddy.

Dinner was a rather awkward affair. It was obvious that Mr. Lee knew every detail about the McKee family. Knew of their debts, of their transgressions of generations past. In her loneliness, Mrs. Paula had turned to writing long letters stuck in thick envelopes.

The town had always wondered where those envelopes were going, and Luella supposed that she was sitting across from the man on the receiving end of it all.

"Aunt Paula says you have the prettiest cows this side of the Mississippi, Mr. McKee," Mr. Jesse Lee said.

It made Daddy McKee's ego warm, a well-deserved treat. "She's bein' sweet on me."

"Don't be silly!" Mrs. Paula smiled. She never stopped smiling, as if she'd smeared her teeth with that fancy petroleum jelly that keeps her hands smoother than a baby's bottom and slicker than a catfish out the water.

Mr. Jesse Lee ate with his wrists sitting against the edge of the table, letting his silverware rest politely along the edge of the fine china. He had a tendency to glance at Mrs. Paula before speaking and nodding while he listened to others talking. He couldn't quite piece together everything Daddy McKee said, that much was obvious.

Perhaps if she pretended her accent was just as thick as her daddy's, he'd grow tired of trying to decode her jargon.

"You're quiet tonight," Mrs. Paula said. "Normally, Luella can tell a joke that will bring the whole congregation down! She's funnier than her father, I reckon."

"It's quite alright. Sometimes I get a bit shy around strangers," Mr. Jesse Lee said.

He spoke to his aunt, but he glanced over to Luella with a glint from his eyes that traveled to the upwards tilt of his lips.

"Mrs. Paula, I'm sitting across from a man who knows God-knows-what about me and I know nothing of him. How do you expect me to act?" Luella responded.

It sent Mrs. Paula into a loud laugh. Her head tilted back so far that her updo threatened to come apart. Luella didn't quite know what she had said that was so funny. Perhaps it was her horrible habit of being truthful.

Mr. Jesse Lee smiled alongside his aunt. "Well, when it gets put like that."

"Luella don't leave no space to argue," Daddy McKee joined in the laughter, letting it shake through his bones. "I hope you're an indecisive man, Mr. Lee."

"Please, Mr. McKee, Jesse is perfectly fine," Mr. Jesse Lee clarified. "And I'm sure it won't be an issue. I like to think I'm rather adaptable."

The comment made Daddy McKee's chuckles continue. While he wasn't too sure originally about Mrs. Paula's kind offers, he was certainly warming up to them. Mr. Jesse Lee seemed nothing like his cousins, and by that point, it was all Daddy McKee felt he could ask for.

Chapter Three

There was only one train station in Crow's Tooth. The train only came through once a week to take out lumber and coal from the neighboring towns. The platform creaked, and in certain areas, the wood had completely rotted away.

Mrs. Paula had a rightful fear of trains, as did Daddy McKee, but he had braved the fear for today. Luella's suitcases, all two of them, were packed full of her worldly possessions. They rested at her feet.

Mr. Jesse Lee stood on the platform, which shook as the train began to arrive. He kept his distance from the father and daughter, giving them their last few moments together.

The train was still on the platform. Mr. Jesse Lee clutched his and his future wife's luggage. He waited patiently.

"I'll catch up with ya soon enough," Daddy McKee promised. "I'll make sure you get a letter from me."

Daddy McKee can't write; he can't read. Old dogs can be taught new tricks, but Daddy McKee is about as human as they get.

Luella didn't have it in her to remind her father of what he could not do.

"I know, Daddy," Luella said, despite the lump of tears behind her eyes. There wasn't much to say, then. The truth was terrifying.

Daddy McKee took a deep breath in, trying to clear the sadness from his mind.

"Alright, dumplin.' Don't lift a finger if you don't have to."

The rule was an odd one, but Luella knew it probably had something to do with Daddy McKee's arrangement with Jesse Lee and his aunt.

"I won't, Daddy," Luella said, keeping a sincere promise out of her voice. She didn't want to make a promise she couldn't keep, especially to her father she may never see again.

They shared one last hug with watery eyes before Daddy McKee helped his daughter up onto the train to the best of his ability. Her hand transferred from his to Mr. Jesse Lee's once aboard the coal-sucking industrial beast.

The sleeping car that had been booked was finer than anything Luella had experienced in her life before. The seats were plush, covered in a soft fabric. The windows were wide and large. From her seat, Luella could see Daddy McKee as he stood on the platform, searching the grimy windows for her.

Mr. Jesse Lee set their suitcases in the designated compartment. Upon noticing Mr. McKee's search, the blonde man reached over Luella with a mumbled *pardon me*. As he leaned over the young woman, his arm grazed the side of her face while he opened the window.

His aftershave was potent. Few men in Crow's Tooth could afford to use the expensive cooling cream, and fewer to wear cologne. It caused her heart to skip a beat. She barely had time to give her thanks before poking her head out the window.

The sound of it unsticking drew Daddy McKee's gaze over. His face lit up upon seeing Luella poke her head out.

"Daddy!" Luella called, even though his eyes were already on Luella. She waved until the train picked up too much speed and was forced to duck back into the car.

The car was silent compared to the platform. The rumble and chug of the beast felt more of a heartbeat.

Next to her, Mr. Jesse Lee set the two train tickets on the table, ready for the conductor to come by and be sure there were no stowaways trying to make it West.

Mr. Lee had also set out a book for the journey. At that moment, Luella felt a bit of shame creep up her spine. Being unable to read and write had never been an issue before, had never hindered her life back in Crow's Tooth. She'd never had to be still for days on end. Normally she was busy from sunrise to sunset. What was she to talk about with a man she knew nothing about?

"Have you been on a train before, Luella?" Mr. Jesse Lee said next to her.

Luella looked over at the man beside her. "No, sir."

Mr. Jesse Lee chuckled. "There's no need for formalities."

Luella let out a little humph. "Formalities are for strangers."

"I suppose we are strangers, aren't we?" Mr. Jesse Lee mused the question over, amused with the defiance.

"I suppose we are," Luella's hostility didn't waver. She felt uncomfortable, and that made her a bit defensive. She crossed her arms like a farmhand would, not a wife.

Mr. Jesse Lee extended his legs out in front of him, deft fingers playing with the tickets atop the table. His hands lacked the calluses of previous suitors, who were few and far between due to the McKee's familial debts.

Luella wanted to ask what the man did, what allowed him to keep his nails trim and his watch crisp and accurate. However, it grated against her morals to give in to her curiosity. The question would open doors that

Luella would not be able to close. She was curious about the man, but did not want to give him the satisfaction of her curiosity just yet.

Instead, she looked away and out the window. She watched as the only town she'd ever known disappeared into the wilderness she'd explored as a child and then into the unknown seas of forest.

The conductor made his way through the cabin. He stopped at the travelers' booths, clipping away at their tickets with his shiny device. Luella watched in curiosity.

The conductor stopped and only spoke to Mr. Jesse Lee.

"Tickets," the man said, holding out his hand.

Jesse Lee passed over the two tickets. The conductor examined them, looking from them to the passengers. He clipped the tickets before returning them to Mr. Jesse Lee.

"Have a good trip, Mr. and Mrs. Lee. Be sure to keep those tickets on you," he said before continuing on.

Perhaps Luella could ask a question. Instead, it came out as a statement, an accusation. "We aren't married."

"The tickets are cheaper for a married couple." Mr. Lee placed the tickets back inside his pocket. "And it's not as if we aren't to be married, is it?"

Luella let out an aggravated huff and looked back out the window. "I suppose."

"I do apologize that we were unable to get married in Crow's Tooth," Mr. Jesse Lee said. Hearing her hometown pronounced without the typical drawl she'd grown up with felt strange, like a new blanket.

It dawned on the young woman that she would never hear that drawl she'd come to love again.

"It's in the past. We can't go back in time," Luella stated. Her jaw clenched, and tears began to well in her eyes upon realizing that she truly could *not* go back in time. That she'd probably never hear from Daddy McKee again, all because her big brother had to go and pretend his pockets were bigger than they were.

Mr. Jesse Lee's Adam's apple bobbed as he watched the woman next to him become overcome with emotion that he could not decode.

He had never been particularly *good* with emotions. His own, and especially with others.

"Do you want me to get some tea brought over?" Mr. Jesse Lee asked.

Luella scoffed. "*Tea?*"

Mr. Jesse Lee gave a hesitant nod. "They do offer tea and water, as well as coffee—"

Luella hadn't had coffee in years. Unfortunately, it wasn't something that she'd been able to afford.

"I'm fine," Luella stated. "But thank you."

The added politeness was a second thought. Mr. Jesse Lee hummed.

"Alright, then. You let me know the moment you need something." He opened his book as he settled in wherever he had left off.

Luella turned her attention back out the window at the rapidly moving scenery. Finally, she settled into her seat, preparing herself for the hours of boredom that were soon to come along with the long and winding journey and her lack of distractions.

Chapter Four

Dinner was served in the dining car. Luella sat opposite Mr. Jesse Lee this time, for which she was endlessly thankful. She tried her hardest to eat as slowly as the man across her, but to no avail. Luella hadn't realized how hungry she had been. She wondered how long the hunger had been building in her stomach.

Her silverware rested atop the empty plate while Mr. Jesse Lee continued to finish his plate. At the gentle clatter, Jesse Lee looked at Luella.

"Here," he offered, swapping their plates with each other. The china clinked through the movements, but no one else in the car paid any mind to the couple.

"I don't want your leftovers," Luella stated, a deep frown slowly setting across her face. The careful movement made her feel like a charity case.

Jesse Lee looked from her to the server, who was already dutifully making his way through the shaking car. How he kept his balance was a mystery to Luella.

"Everything to your liking, sir?" the server asked.

"Delicious, in fact," Jesse Lee stated. "Do you think I could get another plate?"

The server nodded, taking the empty one and whisking it away. Jesse turned back to Luella.

"It doesn't benefit either of us to be hungry."

The new plate was set before Jesse Lee, and he waited until the server turned his back before exchanging the plates again. Before Luella sat a new plate, food warm and presented almost perfectly. She didn't know exactly what the cook had done to the mashed potatoes, but they were some of the best she'd ever had.

Mr. Jesse Lee resumed his now-cool meal, pushing potatoes onto his fork with the help of his half of a bread roll.

"I'm always surprised by how they're able to cook on these trips," Mr. Jesse Lee said. "It's strange, being able to dine so well moving so fast."

"I'm worried I'll leave my stomach miles back," Luella said.

The corner of Mr. Jesse Lee's lip ticked up. "That would be quite a shame, wouldn't it?"

Luella nodded. "Daddy told me I wouldn't have to worry about cookin,' so I guess he's right so far."

"He's definitely right. For living by myself for so long, I should be able to cook, but it's always easier to just pay someone instead. I hope you won't be offended, but Aunt Paula did not have many *good* things to say about your cooking."

Luella wanted to be mad, she really did. However, it's not like she could argue with the truth. She'd almost poisoned Mrs. Paula one year at the church potluck when she was barely a teenager.

Instead, she just sighed and nodded along. "It's alright. I can't say many good things about it either."

Mr. Jesse Lee chuckled, deep and revealing his smile lines. They softened his chiseled exterior.

"You pay your cook, though. Right?" Luella asked.

"I'm a banker, not a barbarian."

Luella chuckled. She turned her head to glance out the window, but the scenery flying by moved far too fast for her.

Everything was starting to flatten out. She'd heard the West was flat but never imagined it would be like *this*. Plains for as far as could be.

"I didn't know Earth could be so flat," she said.

"It's quite insane, isn't it?" Jesse Lee looked out the window. "There's truly nowhere better to see the sunsets, though. When we get home to Oregon, I think you'll be shocked with the scenery there too."

Home. Home with a stranger.

"It's misty most days. And the trees are so big it would take three men to stand around them and hold them. Sometimes it looks like they touch the skies."

Mr. Jesse Lee spoke with such passion about the landscape of his home, such longing for only being gone for a month. Luella was torn between wanting to sympathize with him, wanting to let him miss the scenery he was returning to, and wanting to point out that she'd never get to return to the scenery *she* missed so much.

So, she ate more. It quelled much of the anger that was sloshing about within.

Outside, running alongside the train, was a group of horse riders. The muscles of their horses shone under the sun of the plains. The hooves beat against the dirt, kicking up the dried soil.

Luella had never seen such a thing.

"Is it not dangerous to ride along the track like that?" Luella asked.

Jesse Lee turned his head to follow her gaze out the window. All the relaxation and nostalgia that had been painted upon his face was suddenly gone, replaced by his cold exterior.

"They're more dangerous than the track," Mr. Jesse Lee said. "If we're lucky, their horses are tired."

Luella paled. She had only ever heard whispers about them. Ghost riders, train robbers. Their only loyalty was to their horses and to money. Then, she'd always thought it was strange how much her life mirrored theirs. Loyal to money, loyal to cattle. These horses outside, though, they struck fear into Luella's heart. While most horses feared the sound of the coal-beast's thrumming, these did not.

"Well, the train's faster than a few horses, right?" She glanced over at Jesse Lee, whose attention was focused solely out the window.

He let out a low hum. "We can always hope."

Luella's stomach sank. "That doesn't sound *good*, you know."

Mr. Jesse Lee preferred silence over the truth. So he busied himself with a long drink of his iced tea.

Suddenly, the food before Luella was as unappetizing as her own cooking. Their side of the dining car had become aware of the horse riders thundering alongside the train, with gasps escaping their lips.

Jesse Lee stood from his seat, fixing the nonexistent wrinkles in his button-down. He held out a hand to Luella.

"Perhaps it's smartest if we return to our carriage," he said.

Luella could not help but agree. She took the man's hand in hers, allowing him to help her out of her booth. Jesse Lee let her walk in front of him, keeping close behind her.

As they neared their carriage, a loud *thump* caused them to stumble. Luella reached out for the nearest wall to steady herself. Jesse's hand flew out to grab her hip, keeping her up on two feet while the train came to a halt.

Mr. Jesse Lee cursed. Luella's eyes widened, and she slowly turned her head.

"You can cuss?" she asked, so taken aback by the display of imperfection.

"Is that what you're concerned about right now?" Mr. Jesse Lee asked, furrowing his brows together. His fingers still held her waist.

"It took me off guard," Luella huffed.

Jesse Lee blinked at her in disbelief.

A loud blast caused the entire train to shake. Luella's heart sank deep to her feet.

"We need to get to our things," Jesse Lee reminded Luella, keeping his voice gentle. "C'mon, we're close."

The gentle nudge urged urgency back into Luella's steps. With the train still, her legs shook like a sailor's on land. However, the two of them passed through the cars filled with worried passengers that stood and looked around, bustling in their theories to each other.

Upon entering their private carriage, Jesse took his briefcase down and shuffled through it without grace. He was looking for something in particular.

Luella had nothing of the sort to look through. She stood, watching down the halls intently. A firm gunshot rang out, followed by a ricochet of screams.

Jesse Lee straightened up immediately. He turned to face Luella. Fear thumped at the base of her throat, and her hands shook.

To Luella, the only dangers she had truly encountered were at the hands of animals. Gathering berries and seeing a bear cub and being unable to find their mother. A stressed stallion with overgrown hooves, threatening to beat in the heads of his helpers. The underground thunder from a coal mine collapsing.

Fear had not come at the hands of man.

"What are we to do?" Luella asked quietly. It was the first question she'd asked that withheld the anger she felt at her situation. She could be mad later, when she was either safe or dead.

"Hide, probably. It'll be safest to try and remain undiscovered. We could be days from the nearest town, and it's too bright out to try and steal one of their horses. Which, arguably, I'm sure they planned for."

Luella's already big brown eyes widened more. "Planned?"

"It *is* their job," Jesse Lee reminded Luella. "Come, we shouldn't hide here. Do you need anything out of your suitcase?"

Luella shook her head. "I don't have much to save."

"No books or photos?"

Luella bit her bottom lip in a wash of shame. "I can't read."

"Ah," Jesse Lee said. He took a pause, regarding his bride-to-be. "Your necklace. Is it important to you?"

Luella's hand moved to touch the little locket she had. A gift from her Granddaddy. She nodded.

"Let me put it in my pocket. They'll try to take it from you," Jesse Lee said.

Luella quickly lifted her hands to unfasten the clasp in the back, setting a frown across Jesse's face. He came close to the young woman, reaching his hands around to unclasp the necklace. He placed the thin chain of silver into his inside pocket for safe keeping. At the end of the day, he could always make his money back. A gift as delicate as a locket, however, could not be replaced so easily.

The door to the carriage clanged wood against metal as it was thrown open. Heavy boots hit the carpet. Spurs clinked against the hard, horse-riding heel.

So much for hiding. Jesse removed his glasses from his face, adding them to his growing pockets. He picked up his suitcase, closing the clasps firmly. With one swift movement, the metal corner fastened to his suitcase contacted against the thick window glass. It rang out.

The footsteps in the hall stopped.

Another swing. A large crack began to spread across the window. Luella nervously looked over her shoulder and still saw nothing and no one.

Jesse brought the edge of his suitcase down for the third time. A fourth. The glass gave way just as the door to their private carriage opened.

Standing in the doorway was a shorter man, who held a glistening, silver firearm in his hand.

"Going somewhere?" he asked, voice raspy through the covering of his bandana.

Luella didn't dare turn around. Instead, she kept her gaze trained on Jesse, trained on the spiderweb crack that continued to expand. The three of them stood, frozen in time.

"Honestly, I'm just trying to take my wife on the honeymoon she deserves," Jesse Lee said.

His hand raised, and the gun touched the poof of Luella's hair. A very clear, a very cold warning.

"Don't act like this," Jesse Lee said. He shook his head, slowly beginning to lean against his breaking window. "And it's not like we have anything for you to take."

The robber was unconvinced. "Don't lie to me. This carriage is carpeted."

"My daddy sold his last cow for this," Luella whispered.

The thin brow on the robber arched higher. "His last cow? I have a comrade who calls the women he murders heifers."

"I raise cattle. I ain't one," Luella stated.

Jesse Lee's chest visibly expanded as he sucked in a deep breath.

The robber chuckled darkly. "You think you're funny?" he asked, voice deep and dark. The metal of his gun pressed harsher against Luella's skull.

"She does." Jesse Lee spoke for her. "And she is."

The warm metal moved from Luella's head and pointed at Jesse Lee. The revolver clicked. The bullet ripped through the air, ripped clean through the muscle of Jesse's shoulder, and shattered the window behind him.

"Bad shot." The robber cocked the gun again, aligning it with Luella's head again. The nape of her neck tingled.

Jesse Lee held his wounded arm, keeping it close to his body. They had been so close.

More footsteps were softened by the carpeted ground.

"I want money, not blood," came the voice from down the hall. The robber holding the two at gunpoint turned his head towards the voice.

"I prefer blood over money," the gunholder spoke.

"And I prefer your loyalty over the two."

Jesse Lee inched his good hand over to link his fingers with Luella. He quickly glanced over at the shattered window, then back at Luella. His shoulder was bleeding profusely, tinging his cream button-down with crimson blood.

"Let me finish this," the gun-wielding robber said to the man in the hall.

"Kill them, and you'll have to kill the whole train."

The gunslinging man took pause. His eyes remained trained on Jesse's wound, on

Jesse's blood slowly seeping through the fabric.

"Not even just one?" The lilt in his voice was more akin to a bet than to a request.

The man out of sight spoke. "If they run, then yes."

Pleased with the compromise, the gunslinger sheathed his gun and stepped into the carriage. He opened up Jesse's suitcase, trailing his fingers along the fine monogram by the lock. The suitcase was flicked open without any fanfare, and the man began to go through the neatly packed clothes.

Had fear not been the only thing pumping her blood, Luella would have found it funny that Jesse Lee's suitcase was so neat and organized, much like the man. How telling.

The robber let out a heavy huff upon finding no money tucked between the rich man's clothes.

"There ain't no way…" he mumbled under his breath. He looked over at Luella. "Did the coward hide it in your suitcase? Pull it down."

It took a moment for Luella's instincts to unfreeze themselves. Her hands shook as she lowered the light case and set it down on the table. The gunslinger opened up the suitcase and rifled through it, annoyance rising.

"There's no way you're traveling with no money. Not dressed like that," the gunslinger insisted.

"This isn't my first time on a train," Jesse Lee replied.

Suddenly, a gunshot rang out from further down the train. A whistle and a whoops of excitement followed.

"I'll come back to check on you two later," the gunslinger said as he left the compartment.

There was silence. Neither moved.

Jesse Lee held his arm close to himself, but the wound kept bleeding. It wasn't in any spot that could easily be tied off. Their suitcases sat rifled through on the tables.

With her limbs still jittery from the adrenaline, Luella fought through the frozen reaction to search through her bag. She pulled out the softest material she could find and ripped a strip off.

Then she closed the distance between herself and Jesse Lee, kneeling down next to him.

"We need to wash this out," Luella whispered. "The bugs'll make their home in you."

"We need to get out of here," Jesse Lee whispered. Another gunshot.

"But he promised not to shoot us. He told that other man."

"Do you think robbers are truthful men, Luella?"

Luella swallowed the heavy lump in her throat. The last thing she wanted to do was rely on a stranger, but her choice for independence would leave her dead on the rails.

"They're on horseback, so we need to get a horse to get out of here," Jesse Lee said without much thought. He grimaced as Luella tightened the knotted fabric on his shoulder.

"But they did seem lightly packed earlier…
So we might be closer to civilization than we
realize."

"This isn't your first time being robbed,
is it?" Luella asked. She had wondered why
he had seemed to calm.

Jesse Lee shook his head. He took a
deep breath to collect himself, then stood and
helped Luella up with his good arm.

He poked his head out of the shattered
window. Glass littered the ground below him,
on dirt and rail. On this side of the train, he
couldn't see any horses. He couldn't see any
men.

"They must be on the other side of the
train," Jesse Lee told Luella. He pulled a
blazer from his suitcase and laid it across the
broken windowsill. "We'll hide out there

until they ride off, and then we'll follow the tracks until we reach a town. There's nowhere safe to hide here."

Another gunshot.

"But they know we're here. They'll just keep looking for us," Luella whispered.

"Here we're sitting ducks," Jesse said. "Out there, we at least have a chance."

Against her best wishes, tears of fear welled up in Luella's eyes. "I'd never be in this situation if it wasn't for you."

"Do you want to spend time pointing fingers?" Jesse asked. "Or do you want to climb out of this car and maybe survive?"

Luella bit her tongue. Jesse nodded. With his good arm, he could swing himself over and down from the window, hitting the ground in a crouch to try and dispel the impact.

Another gunshot rang out. Luella looked out the window, hands on the thick fabric. It looked like a far jump.

Jesse stood below the window. He held his hand up to show he was waiting for her, demonstrating how the jump wouldn't be as bad as her anxiety told her.

Luella swung herself over and slid down the hot metal exterior of the train. Jesse caught her by the thighs with his good arm, her dress bunched up and nearly indecent. She was lowered more until her feet could hit the ground and one of her hands rested on Jesse's broad chest.

"Ready?" Jesse Lee whispered. All Luella could do was nod.

He took her hand from his chest, giving it a squeeze. "You can hate me when we're safe, but we have to trust each other until then."

Luella wanted to scoff. She wanted to roll her eyes and run all the way back home to the dark mountains she knew. Instead, she squeezed his hand back and nodded.

Jesse Lee looked around their surroundings. Another gunshot rang out. There was nothing but plains until the horizons. There was nowhere to hide.

"Do you think they'll move the train?" Luella whispered, coming to the same conclusion Jesse was. "We can hide under there."

Jesse swallowed. He wanted to protest, but under the train might be his best and only viable option at the moment.

"Behind a wheel," he whispered.

The two of them crouched and crawled under the oily metal until they were safely tucked away. Gunshots rang out above them. They sat for hours under the metal, groaning and shifting as the bandits roved the halls, merciless with their guns.

They sat for so long that Jesse's arm began to stop bleeding. It was nearly twilight when the two of them heard boots being slid into stirrups. Then they heard the sound of horses clomping about and the bandits rode off.

They sat until the sun had set completely and they didn't need to worry about the bandits returning, hopefully.

Then, in the chill of the night, Jesse Lee helped Luella out from under the train.

Chapter Five

The moonlight was cold. The stars shone brightly. Without forest to obscure the sky, the constellations were completely on display. Luella looked up at them while Jesse Lee looked around.

They were alone. Flies had begun to buzz near the train.

"We need to get you cleaned before they have to take off your arm," Luella said, not looking away from the beauty of the heavens. "And then you'll definitely die. And I can't be unaccompanied."

"Yes, we must," Jesse Lee agreed. "Hopefully, we aren't far from the next town."

They reached the nearest town while the moon was in her highest location across the night sky. Only the inn was still open. Jesse Lee and Luella exchanged glances. Finally, Jesse Lee held the door open for her.

The bell above the door rang, and the bar patrons stopped their conversations to affix their attention on the newcomers. Jesse Lee cleared his throat. "We need somewhere to stay for the night."

The two of them looked like night terrors in the warm lighting of the tavern. Covered in oil, Jesse beat and bleeding. Exhaustion seeping out of them.

"Where do you come from?" The woman behind the bar spoke, cautious and with intention. She was dressed well, with a velvet necklace adorned with a cameo of a rose.

"We were headed back to our ranch in Oregon, but our train got robbed," Jesse Lee explained.

"So you're ghosts," one of the drunkards said. The men who sat with him laughed.

It sent a shiver down Luella's spine. What if they were dead? What if they would be soon? What if because they had survived, they would be tracked down?

The woman behind the bar looked at the drunkards. Then, she glanced down at the bar before looking back to the travelers.

"You got money?" she asked.

Jesse Lee nodded. The woman motioned for them to come over to the bar.

With his good hand on Luella's hip, he guided the two of them over. She didn't dare fight the symbol of possession, not here, not now. She'd hate him later.

At the bar, Jesse was given a key in exchange for a few crisp bills. The woman raised an eyebrow at the money he deposited in her hand.

"It wasn't my first robbery," Jesse said with a friendly smile.

The till rang open, and she slid the money inside. "That much is obvious. Name?"

"Lee. Jesse. And this is my wife, Luella," Jesse introduced them. "What town are we in right now?"

"Gorgor. Missouri," the woman said. "I bet y'all need somethin' to eat. We're closin' up for the night, but I can find somethin' in the kitchen. Bet you need some alcohol."

"Both for drinking and for cleaning," Jesse said, nodding along with the woman. "Thank you so much for your hospitality, Ms..."

"Tilly. You're room four. Up the stairs and to the left. I'll bring it to you," she said.

Jesse and Luella climbed the stairs to their room. Jesse unlocked the door after a few tries. He pushed the door open with a creak, revealing the modest room. A bed, a desk, a chair. Jesse ran his good hand through his hair. Luella immediately flopped onto the bed, throwing her arm over her eyes.

Jesse waited for the food and alcohol to be delivered to the room before he dared to sit down. He knew the second he sat, exhaustion would take over, and his legs would not want to get up without a long night of rest. He took off his tie and his ruined clothes and laid them on the back of the chair. Getting the shirt off without disrupting his wound took a bit of finagling.

At the smell of food, Luella sat up. Her eyes were welled with tears, and Jesse did not point them out. Instead, he poured some of the clear moonshine onto a washcloth and began to dot along his wound with gritted teeth.

Luella looked from the food to where Jesse was tending to his wound.

"Is it bad?" she asked.

Jesse nodded. Luella bit her bottom lip before rounding the bed, coming to his side. She took the cloth and the alcohol from him, dressing the wound to the best of her ability. It was not her first time doing this, as she had done the same for herself for years. Farmhands were always susceptible to injuries.

Relaxed with the moonshine and exhaustion, Luella lay down in the bed while Jesse leaned back in the chair. He claimed it was more comfortable for his wound and kept it raised. Luella felt he was lying and just wanted to be gentlemanly—and she appreciated it.

Then, she slipped into a deep sleep.

Chapter Six

Luella woke to an empty room. The events of the day prior rushed back towards her.

She put her dirty clothes back on and headed out of the room in search of the man she'd come with. There had been a note left on top of her clothes, but Luella had ignored it. It wasn't like she could read it.

The tavern was empty. It wouldn't be filled until the end of the work day.

Ms. Tilly stood behind the counter, dusting. She lifted her head upon seeing Luella make her way down the stairs.

"Your husband headed to the train station to see when the next one is coming through," Ms. Tilly said. "He bought you some breakfast. You want it?"

"Yes, please," Luella said, sitting down at the bar. "What time is it?"

"Nearly noon." Ms. Tilly disappeared through the kitchen doors to grab the woman's meal.

It didn't feel as if Luella had slept for that long. If anything, she felt like she could sleep for hours longer. She was brought stew for lunch, just as it had been for dinner. Luella didn't care. It was hearty, it was filling, it was better than her own cooking.

As she was halfway through her meal, Jesse came back into the tavern. His shirt was new, with no tear or bloodstain on it. He had gotten his wounded arm into a sling, and over his other arm was a dress and a shirt. He paused upon seeing Luella sitting at the bar.

He walked over, setting the shirt and dress down in a neighboring seat. "Good morning, Luella."

"Good morning," Luella responded. "Where have you been?"

"Figuring out what our next step is," Jesse Lee said. "I went to the train station. There aren't going to be any trains coming through here for a few weeks. The tracks are on patrol from the attack. There isn't a train conductor willing."

"Can you blame them?"

"No," Jesse said. "Not one bit. We will be here a while, so I made sure you had some fresh clothes. This is all the seamstress had today that would fit. I sent a quick letter to Aunt Paula to let her know that we were safe and alive. I'm sure word of the robbery will travel back to Crow's Tooth. So, we do have a few options. The general store owner, Dave, is willing to let us stay in his spare room in exchange for some work in the store. We'd also have income for the next few weeks until the next train is finally in."

Luella nodded. "Did you make sure to let Auntie Paula know she has to tell daddy I'm alright?"

"I made sure to include that you were unharmed, very brave, and dressed my wounds. I'm sure she'll tell your father," Jesse said. "We'll just have to make the best of our situation. Which I'm sure won't be too hard. Everyone here seems very kind."

***

Cleaned up and in her new dress, Luella felt like a new woman. Jesse escorted her down the street and pointed out all the stores and homes.

"What time did you leave the room today?" Luella asked.

"I got a late start. Probably around nine?" Jesse said, looking over at her. "Why?"

Luella shrugged. "Seems like you've been up a lot longer, that's all. Since you know so much."

Jesse chuckled. "I just asked some questions. That's all."

The General Store in town was run by the Weavers. It was small, with locally sourced items and a porch out front. Jesse stopped his walk upon seeing Dave sitting on the porch.

He held his hand on Luella's hip, pivoting her towards their new lifeline. She didn't need much prodding, as she understood the reality before her.

"This must be the Mrs. Lee we've heard so much about," Dave chuckled. He had to stand up slowly, hands gripping the wood for stability before reaching his full height. He shook Luella's hand. "You're quite the firecracker, aren't 'cha?"

Luella cast Jesse a look. A *'what have you told them'* look mixed with a *'what have you embellished'* look. Still, she gave Mr. Dave a brilliant smile and shook his hand.

"I don't know if that's the word I would use," Luella said kindly.

Dave Weaver scoffed and began to walk inside. "Aw, I'm sure you're sellin' yourself short. Why don't y'all come on in, and I'll show ya' the fixins'. It's been a minute since we've had long-standin' guests here, ever since the railroads became a huntin' spot. Bandits poachin' on the young. And the rich, but I can' blame 'em there."

The floor creaked under every heavy footstep of the old man. Luella noticed the frightening way Mr. Dave Weaver bore a resemblance to Daddy, the way he walked in accepted pain. The general store he manned was a simple building, with his living quarters on the second floor. He walked slowly up the stairs, each step groaning under him.

It was hot on the top floor, with barely any airflow. The three of them walked down the small hallway until reaching a back room, which Mr. Dave opened with a grunt.

"Knob's a little sticky," he explained, pushing open the door. "It ain't no honeymoon suite, but it'll keep yous on your feet for a few weeks until the future comes to fruition."

The room was rather small, with a little window covered by aged curtains. But still, it was a room. And clearly it was the shop owner's.

"You're too kind," Luella said, recognizing the sacrifice the old shop owner was about to make.

"Ah, it's no problem. I'll bunk up with my brother. You'll be meetin' Norma soon, anyways. At dinner, she's a wild woman! Out in the nature now, but she's ecstatic to have some youngins around. And I'm sure she wouldn't mind an extra set of hands," Mr. Dave said.

"Oh, I don't know if you'd want me in a kitchen," Luella said quickly. "I'm not much good at it."

"Bah, you'll learn," Mr. Dave said. Then, before he took his leave, he turned to Jesse Lee. "Will I be seein' you in a few?"

Jesus Lee gave a polite nod. "Absolutely. I'll be down soon."

"Let y'all little lovebirds have some privacy. I know Ms. Tilly..." He shook his head with a laugh before beginning to hobble back down to the front of the general store.

Once out of earshot, Luella's polite smile dropped and she rounded on her husband-to-be.

"What are you thinking?" she hissed. "We can't share a room."

"Of course not," Jesse said with a frown. "We have a room for the next few weeks, but I'll sleep in the front parlor. And soon, I'll be taking you home. Which, I want to say, is much nicer than this, if that's what you're worried about."

Luella huffed, a bit embarrassed at her outburst.

Jesse opened one of the drawers of the now-empty armoire. He pulled out Luella's little silver locket.

"I did keep this safe for you," he said, offering it to her. "Would you like help fastening it?"

Luella wanted to say no. It would only add to the fact that she would be married to him. Only make it more real in her mind. Instead, she turned around and lifted her brown curls into a fluffy pillow at the back of her head.

He carefully draped the necklace on her collarbone and fastened the clasp on the back, giving it a light tug to ensure it would not fall. Luella's hair dropped and she turned to face him.

She was far too close. She could smell his aftershave mingling with his sweat from his busy day.

"I will see you at dinner," Jesse said. "But I need to go help Mr. Dave move some products to new shelves. When you feel ready, you should come spend time with us. Just to get to know everyone."

Meeting new people was not in Luella's repertoire. She'd known the same people her whole life. Saying goodbye was easier than saying hello.

"However, if you aren't feeling the best, feel free to lie down for a bit. I will make sure you don't miss dinner," Jesse added.

Luella glanced down at the bed behind her before looking up at Jesse. Rest had never been an option for her.

"Travel is tiring," Jesse continued to push the issue. "I feel that this is a town that stays up rather late. Get a few hours of rest for both of us, alright?"

It was impossible to say no. Luella sighed and sat down on the bed. "Are you sure?"

Jesse nodded. "Positive."

"If you need any help, let me know," Luella said. She'd never been this tired before in her life. Perhaps it was the post-train-robbery drowsy.

She lay down so she didn't have to make eye contact with Jesse. So she could let sleep overcome her before it was time to interact with the kind man who was practically a stranger. A stoic, kind stranger who wanted to marry her for some reason.

As Luella waited for exhaustion to comb back over her, she stared at the slats of the wood ceiling. The door clicked shut, and Jesse's footsteps disappeared down the halls.

Chapter Seven

When Luella woke, it was raining. A little drizzle, but enough to keep her in bed. Instead, she lay in the darkening room and listened to the rhythmic pats of water against the tin roof. Footsteps sounded through the hall until the door creaked open. Luella let her eyes slip back shut to pretend to be asleep, wanting to avoid any unnecessary conversation.

"Luella," he whispered. "Hey, c'mon, Luella. You can't sleep through dinner."

Luella pretended to wake up. She took in a deep breath, eyes fluttering open. Jesse's hand stayed on her arm. He was still sweating from whatever work he'd been given while Luella had slept. His hair was pushed back in lightly sweated stands, a little dust of exertion-pink across the bridge of his nose. It was an adorable contrast to the stoic, hard angles of his face.

"Did you rest well?" Jesse asked, voice gentle.

Luella just nodded, her real sleep from earlier still fogging her mind.

"Dinner is going to be served soon. So come on down if you're ready," Jesse said.

Once she collected herself and put her shoes back on, Jesse escorted Luella down the stairs to where the kitchen was tucked away in the back of the shop. Norma was in the middle of a story with Dave, talking and talking and talking. She had short, frizzy hair that was at one point brown but now a fruitful grey.

Distractedly, she ended her story to give the two visitors a warm smile.

"Come in, come in," she invited them through her bustling.

Soon, all of them took their seats. Jesse made sure Luella did not pull out her own seat, much to her side-eye. As a capable woman, there was no need for him to pretend she wasn't.

"Norma, you ain't met Luella yet," Dave said, gesturing between them. His introductions were a bit embellished with age and whatever truths Jesse Lee had stretched earlier.

"I have been hearin' nonstop about you," Norma said, beginning to serve up portions onto plates. "So good to see you in person. I was tellin' the boys about how I'd be just as exhausted as you if I'd had to go through that horrid experience."

"C'mon, Norma, no need to bring it up..." Dave muttered. But a simple mumble could not quell a curious woman.

Luella silently thanked the kind man.

"I just could not imagine having to survive that! You both must be so incredibly blessed to have made it out of there. It's what... Who was it? Jimmy's cousin's brother? Who got stuck on one of those trains, but he was out somewhere scary, was he?" Norma pointed the wooden spoon she was using to serve at her husband while she tried to think about it.

"Nathaniel Hickory," Dave filled in without much hesitation. He took the tool from Norma, standing to serve the food instead of her, letting his wife get lost in storytelling mode.

"That's right!" Norma exclaimed. "Nathaniel Hickory, he got *pillaged* on one of those trips. Of all his things. When his brother went to go collect the body, he didn't have any—"

"There's no need for that kind of horror at dinner," Dave said, cutting off his wife. He, himself, looked a little green.

Perhaps the interruption was more for his sake instead of Luella's. He sat back down with a groan, beginning to dive into the food.

Norma rolled her eyes at her husband's demurity. "Well. It was horrific. Let's just say it's a right miracle y'all's survived. Quite a shock to everyone in the town when you both rolled in. I was catching up with Agatha, which must have been only moments after you left her place." Based on how she briefly turned her attention to Jesse, it must have been him she spoke of. "And she had just sold that dress you have on, Luella. Would not stop talking about all the time he spent tryin' to find one that fit. Trust me, it was something that she should have gone on down and told Wilbur, not me."

Luella glanced over at Jesse, who was focused on his food and his polite attention. She began to eat as well, tucking into the warm food.

"... family friends," she caught Jesse saying. She glanced over at him and tried to put together exactly what he had been answering. "She fell into my lap."

"Just like an angel!" Norma chuckled. "That's what they always say. You must be the luckiest girl in the world, Lue."

How we met, Luella put together. She had to bite her tongue to not refute, because it wasn't like Jesse was *lying*. Aunt Paula and Daddy were friends. She fell into his lap by her brother's mistakes, and now she sat here. In Missouri. Around strangers.

"I'm most definitely guided," Luella said. Mrs. Paula and Norma shared many similarities. One being a softness for Jesse. Luella ate her food and wondered if she was the only woman who didn't fully appreciate the man next to her.

I have different circumstances, is what the young woman finally decided upon.

Chapter Eight

The days blend into a solid routine. Jesse would wake up and then meet Luella down in the kitchen. First, they'd have breakfast with Norma and Dave. Then, Jesse would go to work with Dave, and Luella would clean next to Norma.

Luella always passed by him come mid-morning. She'd wave to him, distract him from whatever he was doing, always to get a wave or a nod of acknowledgment back.

That morning, as she walked through, she was surprised to not see him. She stepped onto the porch, looking down the street to see him in front of the tavern, carrying large barrels of beer into the building.

Luella set off towards him. She picked her dress up as she walked, not wanting to ruin the new fabric. Jesse came back out of the tavern and paused upon seeing the figure coming toward him. Upon recognizing the figure as none other than Luella, he gave her a wave.

She closed the rest of the distance in the time it took for Jesse to load the last of the barrels in. He used a rag to dab away the sweat from his face.

"They puttin' you to work today?" Luella asked, giving Mr. Dave a wave of greeting that he returned. The man slowly began to walk back to his storefront.

Jesse chuckled. "Every day. What are you up to?" he asked. Soon he'd have to head back to the general store.

Luella shrugged. "Just out for a walk. Have you heard back from Ms. Paula?" She asked.

"Not yet. I'm sure we'll get a letter back soon."

The thought of the bandits patrolling the railroad made Luella worry she'd never see that letter. "Are you sure?"

Jesse nodded, giving her a reassuring smile. He rested a hand on her shoulder, giving it a little squeeze. "Mailmen are faster than a train and much more agile."

Luella sighed. "Okay."

"I'll see you tonight," Jesse said. Instead of pressing his lips to her forehead, he pressed the pad of his thumb. He couldn't help but smile as Luella's brow furrowed around it.

"Yeah, I'll see you tonight," Luella repeated.

Jesse parted first. Luella stood for a few moments, with nowhere to truly go. Not with urgency, at least. She placed one of her hands atop her head, which was rather warm.

Continuing her turn about the town, Luella considered if she needed a hat. She wouldn't be here for much longer, and Oregon was cold. Rainy. Not a lot of sun, from what Jesse had described to her. There'd be no use for a hat after this setback, this fiasco.

Eventually, her feet took her out to the pasture. She stood with her arms over the wooden fence, watching the sleepy cattle with a nostalgic yearning. Each one was plump and content, soaking up the sun in the green of the pasture.

Luella couldn't help the jealousy that was bubbling in her stomach.

Chapter Nine

Their nightly routine was normally silent. Jesse was exhausted, and Luella had nothing to say to him. Normally, at least.

However, as Jesse settled by the fire with his book, Luella did not join him. Instead, she crossed her arms and stood in front of him.

Jesse waited for Luella to speak first.

"What if I got a job here to help you out with making some money," Luella suggested.

Jesse didn't even pretend to think it over. "Absolutely not."

Luella's jaw dropped. "What? Why not?"

"It's not your job to do," Jesse said. The spine of his book cracked as he opened it up to one of the pages.

Disbelief filled Luella's face. "I don't understand what your problem is! I was working before, back at home, but I can't work here?"

"Precisely," Jesse said. "I'm glad you're understanding."

Luella scoffed, crossing her arms. "We could leave even faster if we had more money."

"We couldn't, actually," Jesse said. He didn't even look up from his book. "We have to wait two weeks until the next train, anyway. So there's no reason for you to have to worry about anything."

"There's a *lot* for me to worry about right now," Luella said.

"Well, yes, but there's no reason for you *to* worry about any of it. Consider it wife privileges."

Luella let out an exaggerated sigh. "That's so funny you say that, because we aren't married yet. I'm not even your *wife*. I could go get a job if I wanted to. Wife priv—"

Jesse's head shot up. "While we might not be officially married, it is my job to get you back safely to my house. And it is one that I am taking rather seriously. I know you had no choice in this matter, but the least I will do is make sure you get to the life that your father promised you."

Speechless, her heart thudded in her throat. Jesse's shoulders slouched a bit. "I hope you see where I'm coming from."

Luella swallowed. She did not.

"Nothing about you makes sense to me," she admitted.

Jesse looked back up at her. That couldn't do, not when he was going to spend the rest of his life with her. He decided to find a way to cheer her up.

"Have you ever been taken out before?" he asked. "With a suitor?"

Luella tilted her head to the side, thinking it over. She looked off, trying to remember if she *had* any suitors during her time at Crow's Tooth. The only memories that came to her were tarnished by the heavy cloak of her brother's gambling.

"I don't think I've ever had any suitors," Luella said.

Jesse furrowed his brow. "Really? That can't be true."

"Well, it's not as if I've had time. Or pickings. Or the ability," Luella listed off her excuses. "You know about Louis and all of his debts. I couldn't spend any time acting like him."

"Well, would you like to go out tomorrow night?" Jesse asked, eyes set on rectifying Luella's shocking lack of suitors.

Luella sighed as she sat by the fire. "Sure."

It wasn't much of a *yes*, but it turned the corner of Jesse's mouth in a little smile.

He had to make up for breaking the promise of keeping Luella *safe*.

Chapter Ten

Luella hovered about the Weavers' home. While Jesse worked the day away with Dave, Luella had little to do. She walked around the town and passed through the halls. She followed Norma about, but there wasn't much for Luella to do. All the woman did was walk about the town and buy groceries for dinner.

She'd make drinks for Luella to take to the working men, each one cold and with ice. She'd ask Luella to help carve through meat and through vegetables in the kitchen.

At least someone trusted her with some responsibility.

While she prepared vegetables in the kitchen, Luella could not help but notice that it was certainly not enough to feed four of them.

"Are you sure this will be enough for all of us?" Luella asked.

Norma glanced over at Luella. "Just for me n' Dave. Jesse told me this mornin' he was going to take you out for dinner." Immediately, her eyes widened and her eyebrows shot up to her forehead. "Oh, I hope it wasn't a surprise."

Luella blinked. "Jesse mentioned it last night, but I wasn't sure if he was serious."

Relief flew through Norma's body, her shoulders immediately relaxing. "Oh, good. He seemed so excited about it earlier. It's been a long while since Dave and I have done something like that. In all honesty, I hope this wakes him up a little, and we can go have dinner. It's important to enjoy him while he's like this, because one day, he'll just turn into the rest of these old men." Norma let out a loud sigh. Luella wondered how long that rant had been holding inside her.

"I'll keep that in mind," Luella said. She wanted to explain how marriage wasn't her idea, that if anything, she'd prefer a horrible man that she'd feel nothing towards.

Norma looked at her. "You don't sound so excited."

Luella shrugged. "It's just another meal in our lives."

"You two haven't had many meals together, have you?" Norma asked, reaching over Luella for her cutting tray.

"Not alone," Luella said. She thought about their first meal alone, out in the train on the fancy plates.

"I didn't know there were traditionalists out there in the Mountains. Where's home for you, again?"

The simple question meant no harm; Luella knew this. However, it felt like rubbing salt on a wound.

"Crow's Tooth. In Tennessee," Luella said.

Norma let out a low whistle. "You're gonna be far from home. Jesse was right. You are rather brave."

Luella wondered what exactly Jesse said about her when they weren't in the room together. If he was lying about their marital status, what else did he bend the truth about?

"Are you going to go out dressed like that? Go freshen up. You're even prettier put together."

As Luella walked away, she couldn't help but be thankful she was raised by an old man with cataracts.

Over their few days in Gorgor, Jesse and Norma had assembled a small wardrobe for the two of them. Filled with a few donations and the most business the seamstress, Miss Agatha, had seen in years, it gave a little variety.

Luella exchanged her repaired dress from Crow's Tooth that she had refused to get rid of for a floral printed dress. She tamed the frizz in her hair the best she could and repinned it. Her hand shook just a little while doing herself up.

Quick footsteps climbed the wooden stairs down the hall. Luella quickly wondered if she had overdone it.

There was a brief knock at the door before it was pushed open. Jesse stood in the doorway, still sweaty from his workday. He didn't move for a moment while he took in the newer dress that Luella wore. A little smile pulled at his lips.

"You're absolutely beautiful," Jesse said. He closed the door behind him, with one of his hands still behind his back.

"I— Thank you," Luella's voice caught her throat.

Jesse's smile widened. "These are for you, too."

From behind his back, he produced a small bouquet of wildflowers. They were tied together with a scrap of ribbon and twine. When Luella took them out of Jesse's hand, her pinky barely grazed his thumb.

She placed the flowers in a small jar on her dresser, then turned back to Jessie, her cheeks slightly flushed. "Well, shall we go?"

It wasn't until they got to the main floor did Jesse offer his good arm to Luella. She slipped her hand through the link, which made Jesse's chest puff out a bit.

They bid their goodbyes to the already-eating older couple and headed down the street. The sunset went for miles across the sky.

A table within the café/saloon was set aside in the corner, away from the town drunkards and their rowdiness. Jesse pulled Luella's chair out for her.

"If you wait here, I'll go grab us some lemonade," Jesse said.

Soon he was back with two lemonades in mostly clean glasses. "Cheers?"

Luella only lifted her glass to not embarrass Jesse. It made him beam.

"To making the best of situations?" he suggested.

Luella took a deep breath, a little smile creeping onto her face. Their glasses clinked together.

"Do you like workin' here?" Luella asked, genuinely curious.

Jesse nodded. "It's work. And I'm thankful for it."

"I couldn't imagine having so many people know who I am," Luella said. "I never realized how small my town was."

A soft smile tugged at Jesse's heartstrings. "I live in a city, but my house is relatively remote. There will be lots of people there, but you'll have an illusion of there being no one else around."

"I don't know how I feel about that," Luella said truthfully.

"You don't know how you feel about *me*," Jesse pointed out.

Luella raised her eyebrows in reluctant agreement before taking another sip of her lemonade. Food came quickly, and its arrival quelled any conversation.

From his seat, Jesse could see most of the tavern. His eyes quickly zeroed in on one of the patrons. The man stumbled through the sea of tables and bumped into the poker table that was luckily in between games. Jesse's stomach sank upon realizing the man was headed to their table.

He set his silverware down, which drew Luella's attention to him. She looked from his hands to his face.

"What?" Luella asked.

"Hopefully, nothing," Jesse said. He reached under the table and grabbed the underside of Luella's chair, pulling her closer to him. Luella gasped at the display, but was quickly thankful for it.

The man who approached them reeked of alcohol. Luella pulled her drink closer to her.

"Y'know, me 'n' my friends been talkin' bout you," The man slurs. His leer was trained on Luella.

"Go back to your friends," Jesse bit at the man.

The drunkard only chuckled. "Nah, nah, soon. My question is for you." He supported himself on a chair. "How'd you do it?"

"How did I do what?" Jesse asked.

"You know. I wish I had a wife like that. I know I could treat her better." The man looked over at Luella. "I've seen you around town, walking alone. You ain't wearing no ring, and I'm thinking maybe you ain't even married at all."

Jesse blinked at the man. "Excuse me?" he asked, voice low and dangerous. He stood, fists clenched tightly.

"In fact," the man said, "I think maybe you ought to try a different man, since you ain't hitched to this one." He reached out to Luella, who stepped back in fear.

In a flash, Jesse stepped forward and swung a solid punch to the man's jaw. The drunkard fell to the sticky floor, and Jesse stood over him.

"Do not ever speak of her like that again," Jesse warned. Then he led Luella out of the tavern without looking back.

Chapter Eleven

The Weavers had long since gone to bed. It was completely silent as they entered. Instead of turning on any of the gas lights, Luella located a long candle and lit it while Jesse went to find some bandages and alcohol. He had busted his knuckles on his punch and was bleeding.

Once sat at their makeshift infirmary at the table, Luella quickly set about cleaning the wound out. Jesse hissed at the alcohol.

"You know," Luella said, focused on her work. "You give *horrible* first impressions."

Jesse chuckled through the stings. "I do have my shortcomings."

Luella carefully wrapped the clean bandage around his hand. "You just came across as very… Stuck up."

"I have been told I'm too serious," Jesse agreed.

"Well, I'm not sure if seriousness is bad," Luella said. "However, stuck-upness…"

"A different story entirely, I understand," Jesse said. As Luella finished tying off the dressing, Jesse gently flexed his hand.

There was a pause. Luella watched Jesse get used to the new bandage.

"How does it feel?" Luella asked.

"Perfectly fine," Jesse assured her. He looked up from the wound to the woman across from him. "I didn't mean for tonight to go like this."

"I couldn't tell."

Jesse couldn't help but smile at that. Her voice softened. "You've gotten pretty beat up over the last few days."

Jesse shrugged. "It has been a long time since I've gotten injuries. I suppose I'm making up for lost time." He looked at Luella. "I hope I haven't scared you. I'm not a violent man."

What a ridiculous statement. Compared to the men on the train, Jesse was not violent. Compared to the Galloway Boys back home, Jesse was not violent.

"You think I find you violent?"

Jesse nodded.

Luella rolled her eyes. "I don't know what kind of bubblegum valley you've been living in, but you aren't. At least, I hope so. You've been nothing but kind to me as of late."

Jesse's lip twitched in an amused way at her figures of speech. "A bubblegum valley?"

"Yes," Luella said, immediately rising to her defenses. Jesse's smile began to take over his whole face. "Don't make fun of me!"

"I'm not, I'm not," Jesse promised. His smile still remained. "I've never heard that before. It's sweet. I might have to use it."

He changed the topic. "You know, it's a shame I never got to tell you how beautiful you look tonight."

"It's still nighttime," Luella whispered.

Jesse leaned forwards. "Well, you look absolutely stunning tonight."

The blush that crept across Luella's face could not be helped. Nor could the smile that spread across her face at the genuine compliment.

"Thank you, Jesse," Luella said. She didn't know when it had become so easy to call him by his name.

"It's my pleasure, Luella." Jesse didn't dare move from the warm candlelight, despite exhaustion creeping up on him. Their hands rested millimeters from each other.

Chapter Twelve

Eggs were already sizzling in the pan, not quite ready to be put onto a plate before Norma began her morning inquiries. Dave held onto his last few moments of sanity while sipping dark, black coffee.

When Jesse entered the room, he was the last one to arrive. Everyone turned to look at him. To everyone's surprise, Luella was the first to greet him.

"Good morning," she said, already removed from her cooking duties.

"How was last night!" Norma asked, glancing briefly over her shoulder. She watched as Jesse sat down next to Luella. "Seems to have done you both an awful lot of good."

"It was good to get out," Jesse elaborated. He rested his hands on top of the table politely.

Dave glanced up from his paper. "What happened to your hand?" he accused more than asked. "Ain't that your good one?"

Jesse glanced over at Luella before looking back to the man. "I got into a bit of a scuffle last night."

Norma gasped and brought over eggs for everyone at the same time. "A scuffle? Are you alright, dear?"

"You should see the other guy," Jesse said.

"What happened?" Norma asked, shaking salt and too much pepper onto her eggs. She sneezed before diving into her meal.

Jesse and Luella exchanged a look before Luella turned back to her food.

"One of the drunks came up to us and has some impolite words to say," Jesse said.

It was the Weavers' turn to exchange a look.

"Don't skimp out on us," Norma encouraged. "What did he say?"

Jesse cleared his throat. He glanced over at Luella, who was more interested in pushing her food around than being involved in the conversation. "He claimed we aren't married."

Norma's eyes got wider than they already were. "No, you have to be pulling.'"

"No, ma'am," Jesse said. "I wish I was. Horrible end to the evening."

"What a silly comment to make! You both *are* married, aren't you?" Norma further inquired.

Luella's heart rate sped up beyond belief. She swallowed a thickness in her throat, one that definitely wasn't eggs. She could feel Jesse's eyes on her before they quickly shifted off.

"We were supposed to get married in Oregon," He admitted.

A ringing silence coated the table. Norma's face transferred from shock to excitement in moments. Finally, she let out a giddy little laugh.

"Oh, we *must* do something about that!" She said, excited like a honeybee in a patch of daisies. "You should have said something earlier. There is no reason for happiness to wait for a train! We'll throw you something together, right Dave?"

The older man just nodded along with his wife. However, there was a glint of happiness in his eyes at the news.

Once breakfast was cleared, Norma quickly whipped everyone into motion. She convinced Dave to close the store for a few hours for the happy event. She turned down all of his grumblings and bemoaning about lost business with a sharp, "Don't act like that. I remember just how happy you were on *our* wedding day. Jumpin' up and down these same streets. Hypocrite in your old age is all you are."

Jesse stayed in the kitchen with Luella to help her with the washing so Norma could iron Luella's dress.

"You'll have to sign your name," Jesse said to Luella, passing her a wet dish for her to dry.

"If I just scribble something, will that work?" Luella asked. "I never had to sign my name before. I don't know how to do it."

"That's alright. We can practice before we head down. You should know how to sign with McKee before you get a new last name." Jesse spoke so nonchalantly about it all that Luella had to hold extra tight onto the plate to be sure not to drop it and instead place it back in the cupboard.

"I can't believe you ended up being nice," Luella said. It made Jesse laugh over the soapy sink.

With the dishes done and some paper and a pencil stolen from the front of the store, Jesse and Luella sat at the table.

"They'll probably have you sign with ink, but this will work just fine for practice," Jesse said. Very carefully, he held the pencil between his fingers before handing it to Luella. His fingers were feather-light as he corrected her hold.

Once Luella had her grip down, he covered her hand in his and swept the pencil through the looping motions of her maiden name. They sat there, with Jesse's aftershave full in her senses and his hand over hers until the loops felt natural. Until he could take his hand off of hers, and she could perform the motions all by herself.

"And Lee is very easy," Jesse said. "All you do is take the L from your first name and add the e's from your last."

He only had to guide her through his last name once before she understood it.

The scrap of paper decorated with many tries of Luella's name sat before them. Jesse looked at the piece of paper with soft eyes.

"I'll teach you soon," Jesse promised. "This will have to do for now."

"I just hope you aren't embarrassed," Luella mumbled. She, in fact, was.

"Luella," Jesse said. When she didn't look up at him, he gently placed his finger under her chin and nudged her. "If I was embarrassed by you, we would not have made it this far. When we're done at the courthouse, we can go on a real date, without anyone trying to disturb our peace."

A bashful smile crept across her face, quickly followed by a blush. "Okay. That sounds nice."

Jesse wanted to lean in and kiss her forehead. He'd be able to in a few hours.

The sheriff ended officiating the marriage. He had to dig a spare marriage record from the bottom of his cabinet and shake the dust off of the thick paper.

"Ain't no one been married here in a while," he chuckled, signing his name on the officiant line before handing it to Jesse to sign first. "Gorgor ain't exactly a fancy town."

Jesse smiled as he signed. "It wasn't in our plans either, but we couldn't be happier."

He slid the paper over to Luella, gently placing the pen in her hand. Her hold was a little sloppy, but she was able to complete the swirls of her name easily, with no problem.

"Alright, we just gotta let this dry, but y'all are good to go. Mr. and Mrs. Lee, huh," the sheriff said, shaking his head.

Luella could feel the expectant eyes of the Weavers on them.

"Kiss her!" Norma urged.

Jesse just chuckled and looked down at Luella. "Is that alright with you?" he asked quietly, like a secret. His good arm with his bad hand was already weaving around her waist.

Luella gave a little nod. Her heart raced in her chest. *What if I'm bad at it?*

Jesse closed his eyes and Luella followed suit, and soon her senses were filled to the brim. Gentle lips moved against hers for just a few brief moments. It was a rather strange sensation.

And when Jesse pulled away, Luella wanted to pull him back in.

The End

FREE GIFT

Just to say thanks for checking our works we like to gift you

Our Exclusive Never Before Released Books

100% FREE!

Please GO TO

`http://cleanromancepublishing.com/gift`

And get your FREE gift

Thanks for being such a wonderful client.

Please Check out My Other Works

By checking out the link below

http://cleanromancepublishing.com/fjauth

Thank You

Many thanks for taking the time to buy and read through this book.

It means lots to be supported by SPECIAL readers like YOU.

Hope you enjoyed the book; please support my writing by leaving an honest review to assist other readers.

.

With Regards,

Faith Johnson

Printed in Great Britain
by Amazon

41019281R00078